THE GARGOYLICON

IMAGININGS AND IMAGES OF THE GARGOYLE IN LITERATURE AND ART

Published by
Mind's Eye Publications™
985 Deborah Avenue
Elgin, IL 60123-1918
mindseye.pub
mindseye.us.com

Front Cover Art by Lee Murray
Back Cover Art by Kyla Lee Ward
Cover Design & Lettering by Frank Coffman
Edited by Frank Coffman

MIND'S EYE

PUBLICATIONS

ISBN: 978-1-7367114-8-4
Trade Paperback$10.00 US Print

The Gargoylicon

Imaginings and Images of the Gargoyle in Literature and Art

PUBLISHED 30 APRIL 2022

EDITED BY
FRANK COFFMAN

Dedication

To that inigmatic figure—

The Gargoyle

· Functional Protector of
Gothic Structures,
· Fearfull Visage to
Ward Off Evil
·Beckoner of Pagans
to Join a New Faith
· Frightening Stimulous
for Righteousness and Piety

Table of Contents

INTRODUCTION

THE GARGOYLE is often associated with Medieval architecture, but there are examples going back to ancient Egypt and Greece (around the temple of Zeus, for example)—where, in each of those cultures, the lion's head was the typical form. The name almost certainly derives from the Latin *gargula* ("gullet" or "throat").

But the association with the Middle Ages and Gothic architecture is strong. Gargoyles and Chimeras bedeck many Medieval churches. Likely the most famous are those of Notre Dame in Paris. While the great majority of gargoyles are draconifom grotesques, many examples exist depicting other animals and even humans. The key feature is that their practical use is as a water spout to send rain water safely away from the walls and base of an edifice.

The notion that the Gargoyle might be alive or even become animated—Or the reverse of that! In one French legend, St Romanus, Bishop of Rouen (fl. c. 631-641 A.D.) related how he rid the country of a monster known as *La Gargouille* by subduing the fire-breathing dragon with the aid of a crucifix and but one man who volunteered to assist. The tale goes that they burned the carcass, but the neck and head would not burn, having been tempered with its own fire. The neck and head were then mounted on the wall of a newly built church to ward off evil spirits. Sound familiar?

There is a split theory about the views the Catholic church took about the gargoyle. One theory holds that they represent the powers of Evil to be rightly feared. Another, opposing view sees them as apotropaic devices used to ward off Evil. Some see their use as an added incentive to the unconverted to come to the church, while giving a nod to the beasties of their pagan past, at the same time offering the protection of the church.

The creatures were often anthropomorphized and legends arose about their possible sentience and even mobility!

In any event, the fiction, poetry, and illustrations contained within this tome present reflections upon, re-imaginings, and a fine spectrum of perspectives and approaches to these most intriguing grotesques of stone.

We hope the reader enjoys this cornucopia of visions and interpretations of the Gargoyle in Literature and in Art.

Frank Coffman, Editor
Elgin, Illinois
26 April 2022

GARGOYLE

by Manuel Arenas

How many years have I crouched upon my haunches on this corbel, overlooking the roofs of this tiny village? Who knows; who tracks time but mortals? I have borne the wind's great gusts, with its once refreshing, but now fetid breath; as well as the torrential rainstorms that have lashed about my face, mocking my immobility. But I have endured it all with indifference, for I am imperturbable.

I am a sentinel placed here centuries ago, by men long gone, for a purpose long forgotten by their scions. Forsaken but undaunted, I continue in my service: the duty of guarding these creatures from the ever-present cloud of darkness that hovers over their fragile little heads. Waiting for a chance to slip into this plane from its netherworld of chaos to wreak havoc and obfuscate the eyes of the masses with its visions of wickedness and self-importance.

Preying first on the weaker minds, whose already opaque eyes will be the first to be blinded by its lies. Those whom are strong willed, and resist, will be struck down like bothersome pests, not to be tolerated, much the lass feared.

Thus, I await the day with much anticipation when my companions and I shall answer to the call to battle the legions of the dark. Only then shall we have fulfilled our promise to the long-forgotten masons of our visage.

GARGOYLES AND GROTESQUES V. 3.0

Kathryn Reilly

Gargoyles graced powerful empires:
stone masons' homages to
the fiercest known and imagined creatures
protecting sacred buildings from Seth
and honoring Zeus and Jupitar's temples
throughout the great civilizations of Egypt, Greece, and Rome

Kayseri, Turkey claims the oldest guarding gargoyle
whose crocodilian gaze has weighed humanity
13,000 years and counting; yet humanity
lost interest in all creatures,
their imagination falling fallow, longing for inspiration

Version 2.0 emerged as Christianity's dominion
claimed medieval Europe carving gothic guardians
adorning churches closest to heaven,
protecting sacred stone, fending off evil,
reminding its faithful to choose goodness
lest their souls mirror their grotesque insides—
fear of unknown lurking evils crafted
monsters constantly watching

Version 3.0 evolved as science reigned
and pop culture, the craziest cousin, demanded
modern icons replace their crumbling ancestors;
look skyward to find Hollywood's finest:
France's Chapelle de Bethléem
proudly boasts Gremlins and Gizmo,
Aliens' xenomorphs, the robot Grendizer;

Scotland's Paisley Abbey hosts
an *Aliens'* xenomorph as well;
England's St. John the Baptist Church in Cirencester
shares a punk rocker while Ely Cathedral across the way
offers a proud nose picker (every mother's fear);
Washington National Cathedral
hosts a gas-masked creature alongside
Darth Vader's grotesque: modern evil incarnate

No longer apotropaic, these latest
versions celebrate human
imagination and universal possibility once again

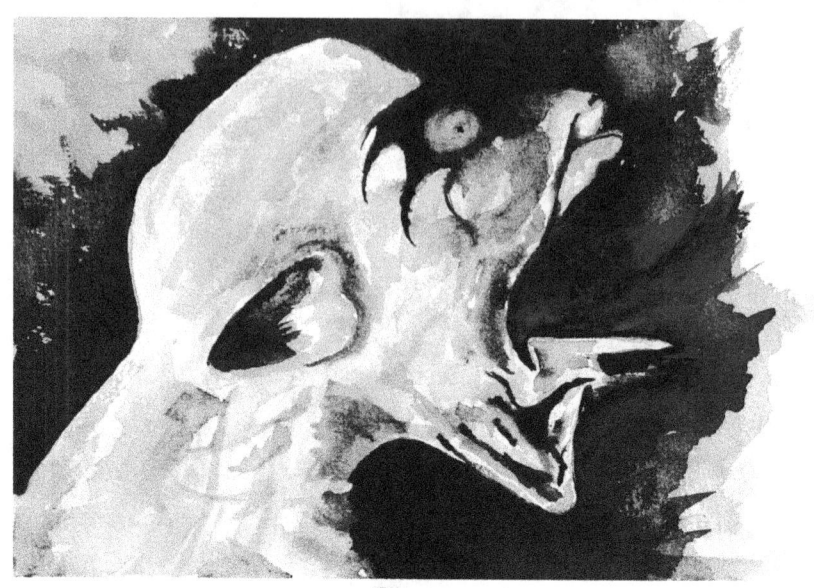

CURSED

Lee Murray
(both illustration and poem)

Hunkered hideous on this grey façade
A gargoyle, an abhorrent stone grotesque
Where hail and sleet and century corrade
These lonely years, I've spouted in protest
A woman locked me in this bitter hell
As I'd not wed one with a face so vile
Poor victim of that spiteful witch's spell
Because my princely blood I'd not defile
Then came you, to beg for blessed sanctuary
When ignorance would burn you for your skill
A kiss was all I asked to help you flee
My love, you gave it gladly; t'was your will

Broke from the curse, restored, I'm free to roam
Now you're the one condemned to angel-stone

Miss Anna's Gargoyle

Marge Simon

Anna was born sickly and lame, with a large red birthmark on one cheek. She was next to youngest of twelve children, and her mother had no time for sympathy. "Don't come crying to me about their teasing, Anna. You're an ugly little girl, deal with it. You may as well pick a fight with the sky because you don't like the shade of blue.

So be it. Anna accepted reality. When she was fourteen, a young man with yellow hair and a sparkle in his eyes asked her for a stroll. Disregarding her mother's warning, she donned a cloak and met him at the door. As she soon found out, a friendly stroll was not his grand intention. Bloodied and bruised, she limped home.

When she was old enough, she went to work as a kitchen maid on Bell Yard Street in Mrs. Lovett's Pie Shop. Anna's main job was to make the pastry and par boil the meat for the pies. The meat was always fresh and cut into chunks from non-descript parts of the sheep when it arrived. At least, Anna assumed it was from a sheep, or sometimes a cow. Mrs. Lovett's lover. (she called him "Sweetie") was Sweeney Todd, the town barber. He procured the mutton or beef, whichever it was. He also helped with the butchering and disposed of the bones. Such activity was always done very late after Anna was in bed. Sometimes she wondered why Todd brought it in through an underground passage next to her own little room. Every other eatery had the meat delivery by horse and cart to the back door. But this was none of her business, so she kept such questions to herself.

With that unsightly birthmark and limp, townsfolk avoided her company. She had no friends. When she passed townsfolk on the streets, she knew what they were saying.

"There goes that poor girl, works for Mrs. Lovett. What a strange one she is!"

"That's got to be the ugliest creature in London, don't ye know it!"

"Even old *Rawhead and Bloody Bones* wouldn't want her!"

Wednesday evenings, she was allowed to attend prayers and Confession at St. Dunstan's church. One night, Anna was feeling especially sad afterward. The only sin she could come up with was not thanking the Almighty enough for her health and food. Once outside, the moon was unusually bright, casting light on the church's single gargoyle. Such a hideous, terrible thing it was! Just like her, Anna thought. stuck in one place until it crumbled and fell to earth. Sobbing, she found her way to the stairs in the alley. Driven by thoughts of suicide, she climbed to the highest point in the roof.

There at the edge, she trembled as she looked down, one hand on the gargoyle. Of a sudden, she felt it move. Was it looking at her? Did one of its eyelids actually wink at her? Unmistakably, it winked again. Slowly she stepped back from the edge and hugged it tightly. For the first time in her life, she was at peace. Moreover, she was sure it would come alive only when no one was looking, and it would do so for her alone. Nights to follow, she brought it chunks of bread and cheese. As it ate, she gently stroked its fearsome forehead. Eventually, she told it her story, for surely no person cared to hear it. A tear came to its bulbous eye. It licked her fingers. "Someday, somehow – we'll escape this place. We'll make a world of our own," she whispered. Its huge eyes turned spinach green and narrowed.

Now it so happened that this sad gargoyle had a story of his own. His grandsire was a fierce dragon back in the days of King Arthur when Magic ruled. According to legend, his name was Belchur and he ravaged the town of Camelo. Eventually, Merlin crippled him with a spell and his body was slain and burned. Yet

The Gargoylicon : Imaginings and Images

before his death, he had mated with a griffin, and fathered a fair number of hideous offspring, later known as gargoyles. Of course, in those times, such creatures were too dangerous to allow their freedom. Thus, the lot were cursed by their sire's misdeeds, and ensorcelled sit on churches for centuries after, unable to fly. Their unlikely liberation would be possible only if kissed by an innocent.

Old Silas happened to be propped up on a wall across from St. Dunstan's Church one evening. He claimed he saw the gargoyle leave the roof. It was midnight, the moon was full, and he swore it swept down through the window of Sweeney Todd's barber shop. A moment later, it soared back out. But Silas was the town drunk. When he added that he was sure a young woman was riding on its back, the townspeople walked away laughing.

True, the old gargoyle on the church roof was missing, but most folks didn't even remember it was there in the first place. Concerning Mr. Sweeney a.k.a. "Sweetie" Todd – once the constabulary came to address the damage to his shop, they discovered the trap door hidden under his barber chair. In the cellar was the body of a new victim. As for Anna's disappearance, Mrs. Lovett never mentioned it. She certainly had enough to deal with when the truth came out about the kind of meat in her pies. But that's another story.

Gargoyle People

Bruce Boston

If gargoyle people
were the world,
standards of beauty
would be far different
than they are today.
The eye of the beholder
would adore the grotesque,
worship the malformed,
rejoice in the appalling.

We would stand still
for hours at a time
without flinching,
never blinking,
glaring into one
another's countenances,
baring our static rage
and indomitable horror
with pride for all
the world to see.

When shadows of the sun
or moon moved across
the lines and planes
of our chiseled faces,
umbra and penumbra
like shifting scars,
we would celebrate the

hideous chiaroscuro
that light and its
absence invoked.

The rains would darken
our expressions further,
mottling our features
like a pox, sending
the dirt from Heaven
coursing through our
orifices in torrents,
spewing from our mouths
and staining our lips
in muddied streams.

And when the winds
teased our cracks and
crevices and whistled
and thrummed through
the stone hollows
of our wrathful selves,
the music we would
make would be fierce,
lovely, rich, and mad.

(Appeared in *Asimov's SF*, April/May, 2008)

GARGOYLE LOVE SONG

Joshua Gage

They say that I was carved to wait forever.
What do they know? I was born of snow,
cold wind, and stone. It took me the better
part of a millennium to grow
this still, this old. I lurked above the holy
doors, waiting for love to sweep into
my life. I did not think you would be rosy
pink. But you winked at me. I knew you knew.
I watched you age with week and year until
wrinkled, slow, and weathered—a perfect mate.

One day they brought you to me, gift-wrapped, still
and silent. But you were planted, and so I wait
for you to grow from out the ground, join me
and fly. I'll wait forever. I'm good at waiting.

"Gargoyle Love Song." Twilight Times.
http://www.twilighttimes.com/oct02/j_Gagep18.html

TERROR INCOGNITA

Liam Spinage

"This is what's known as the basin room." Marc's voice rang out loud in the subterranean chamber, in part to make sure he could be heard over the sound of the slow but heavy dripping of water and in part because he rather liked the sound of it. That's what a tour guide should be like, he would instruct the new team members, loud and clear and unafraid of their own narrative.

Far behind him, not yet at the entrance to the room, two late arrivals to the Paris Catacomb tour struggled to hear him, not because of the volume, but because they were busy bickering with each other.

"You know I didn't want to come down here and now look, I've got mud all over my skirt. Honestly, Bill, can't we just go? Let's go back to that nice cafe we saw a couple of streets back and spend the afternoon there instead."

Maisie's eyes were pleading, but Bill couldn't see them in the pitch dark of the tunnel. He fiddled with his headlamp for the third time and pretended not to listen.

"Bill?"

"Oh, they say not to wander off on your own down here. Didn't you listen? That was the first thing the guide said. We might get lost. There's over two hundred miles of…"

Maisie cut him off. Bill could be a walking tour all on his own, they didn't need a guide. "We could cut back easily enough. The tunnels are lit most of the way. Pl-ee-ase."

"Spooked out are you?" This wasn't spoken out of concern, nor entirely out of mockery. Truth be told, Bill himself was more spooked by the catacombs than he'd thought. They'd already tramped through passages lined with skulls and the guide had done his utmost to convey a ghostly atmosphere, with his little vignettes about people going missing and never being found again. Not that he could admit that, this had been his idea and they were damn well going to enjoy it, thank you very much. Though, he thought in reflection, perhaps more ;endure' than ;enjoy;.

He looked over at Maisie, who was trying to scrape mud away from a sunflower yellow skirt and only making it worse. It would look awful when they hit sunlight again. That would be his fault as well. Perhaps there was something in being lost down here alone forever after all, he mused.

"Come on. We'd better catch the others up. They've already moved out of the room, I can hear their feet shuffling. Don't want to get lost."

Maisie was thinking she would very much like Bill to get lost. Nevertheless, she shuffled on, eager to be back out in daylight with a nice glass of wine and a view of the Seine where it was beside or beneath them, as it should be, and not seeping through the walls around them.

They both emerged into a room that was empty now and stone-cold silent. A shimmering of lamps trailed away through an arch opposite them just as they entered.

If the bone-lined passageways had spooked them a little, this room was something else. Not the natural curves of the soap-stone tunnels, here was a great stepped pool in the middle of the room fashioned by human hands. Graffiti spat angrily from the walls of the cave in splotches of red and yellow, lit only by their meagre headlamps now. Before them crouched a great gnarled statue, bent over the pond in a crouch. A small rivulet of water poured constantly onto its head through the roof above and exited through its mouth into the pool. In other settings, above ground in a garden maybe, this picture might have been serenity itself. Below the streets of Paris, it was nothing less than terrifying.

Bill let out a little gasp, then stifled himself so as not to appear too afraid.

"Well, hey there, fella." His half-joking attempt to address the gargoyle was an attempt to steady his nerves. He failed. "Don't suppose you know where the others went, do you?"

Silence. Obviously. Emerging beside him, Maisie also gasped, though hers was quite different.

"Oh wow. Look at that! What a wonderful work of art!"

Bill turned slowly, incomprehensibly. His eyes rolled and his eyebrows raised, not that Maisie could see, What light they had between them was focused solely on the scene ahead.

"I wonder where the water drains to?" Bill, an engineer by profession, always tried to address the nuts and bolts of a situation. Especially if it detracted from the ugly face staring back at him in the gloom. Maisie, an artist, was much more inclined to be lost in the moment. She sloshed her way through the muddy floor to stand beside the gently stirring waters of the pool and dipped a hand in. It was almost unnaturally cool. She hoisted her shoulder bag round to the carved lip of the pool beside her and began to search for something inside.

"Uh, Maisie, we really can't stay here, We've got to catch up with the tour."

Maisie apparently wasn't listening. She'd pulled a sketchbook from her bag and began fishing for her sketching pencils which she knew were buried in there somewhere.

"What do you want to draw that for anyway? It's grotesque!"

"Nope, not grotesque." Maisie was in her element now and began lecturing. "It's a gargoyle. Grotesques don't have the water-spout, that's what makes the difference. Come and look! They look like they're fashioned after the gargoyles on the Notre Dame!"

Bill groaned, took a brief look down the tunnel where he could still just about hear the low drone of their guide, and groaned again.

"Fine. It can't be that hard to catch up with them anyway, all those feet tramping around are bound to leave footprints in this mud. Just don't be long."

Maisie allowed herself a little smile and patted the rim of the pool next to her as if offering Bill a seat while she worked. Bill preferred to stand rather than get any more of his clothes damp, so he declined and did a little tour of the room instead, trying to decipher the graffiti with his poor French and failing at almost every word. He gave up quickly and leaned against a dry portion of the stone wall, thumbing the guidebook in the dim light of his headlamp.

Maisie set out three pencils and an eraser beside her and began to sketch, pointedly ignoring Bill. She had to admit he'd had a good idea when he suggested this tour though. She was beginning to enjoy herself immensely.

What was that? A flicker of light in the corner of her eye. She looked up suddenly, expecting Bill to have moved from the wall, about to cast everything back into realms of dark shadows. He hadn't moved though. She looked back at the gargoyle, determined to capture its facial expression from vestigial horn through to fanged mouth, just as whoever carved it had. Background detail could wait, it was the foreground that mattered here, the fine interplay between motes of shadow and light that...

She hesitated. The gargoyle had closed its eyes. She dropped a pencil in alarm and fumbled for it on the muddy floor. When she looked up again, its eyes were once more wide open.

A trick of the light. Nothing more. Still, she'd be done here soon. Then she could take a couple of photos to help her fill in the rest of the pool and cavern later.

Had its paw just moved? No. Couldn't have been. Still...

"Bill, come here would you? Take a look at this."

Bill ambled over. He looked bored rather than impatient.

"What's up? Oh! It's sitting up straighter now. That's odd." He said 'odd', but what he meant was 'very disturbing indeed'. He didn't let it show.

"It is? Maisie looked up from sketch to subject. He was right. It did look like it had moved again slightly.

"Perhaps it's waiting to devour us!" Bill was trying to be funny to counter the feeling he had in his throat, but it came out with the tone of terror that was in his heart, not the one he wanted on his tongue."

"It's just the way it's lit up. I need a static light source rather than this torch in my wobbly off-hand. If you'd be so kind?" She handed it over to Bill, who held it firmly. "Besides, gargoyles don't eat human flesh." She said this in such a matter-of-fact voice that Bill found it more frightful than when it echoed around them.

"Oh, they don't? Well that's a relief!" Bill did not sound relieved. Everything was telling him to leave this place now.

"They're for protection. They're ugly to scare off evil spirits."

"You really are a mine of information! Really though, it's time we..."

"Oh, I'm done. There!" She turned her sketchbook round to show Bill her handiwork. "Not bad for ten minutes! Here, help me up, would you?"

"Do not move."

Neither of them were quite sure in that moment where that voice came from. The sudden volume shattering their solitude and the many echoes which followed rendered them both to blind and immediate panic. Maisie dropped her sketchbook, Bill dropped the torch. They both landed unceremoniously in the pool, causing little ripples on the surface which crashed against those caused by the slow drip from the gargoyle's mouth.

It is, after all, not a sensible thing to say if you really want people not to move. It invites them to jump up immediately, to flee if they can, to cower in a corner. What it doesn't do is actually encourage people to stay still. But the owner of that voice was beyond such concerns.

"Stand up. Slowly. Then turn around."

Simple instructions. A much better solution.

"Walk over to me. Again, very slowly. We don't want to disturb the statue."

A figure emerged from the opposite archway. It wore the exasperated expression of a tour guide who really had better things to do than babysit every damn tourist that didn't listen.

To his surprise, they both complied, and rather quickly. Looks like they were spooked already.

"You opened yourself to much danger, remaining here when we all left. Do you realise that?"

He sounded sincere. Only Marc knew the smirk that lay hidden behind those words.

"The statue, you see. It moves. It would catch you and then you would be lost here forever."

"Maisie says that gargoyles are good guys. Right Maisie?"

Marc was amazed they were actually buying this. He decided to extend his little joke on them a moment longer.

"Not the gargoyle. The walker-through-walls. Look! Over there!" Marc raised his torch theatrically. On one section of the wall Bill hadn't explored was a horrific sight. Trapped half in the wall of the chamber was the form of a man, his face and arms extending out toward them.

"He would have had you both. Luckily, I was here to rescue you." Marc adopted a pose meant to indicate bravery and pride, but which came across as arrogance. "Now, please follow me. And stay close this time. We don't want any incidents, do we?

Maisie and Bill looked at each other, then nodded agreement. Whether or not there was any truth in the tale of this mover-through-walls coming to get them, they were both done with being spooked out for today and a good few more days besides.

As they left, Maisie turned round briefly to say farewell to the gargoyle squatting over the pool. As she did so, she noticed in the dim light that it had one eye firmly shut and the other open, as if it was winking at her but was caught in the moment.

She wasn't sure what that meant, but she decided not to think about it until at least they'd finished their first bottle of wine.

Immobile No More

DJ Tyrer

Bulging eyes watch
Congregants entering church below
Pious frauds, confessional cheats
Gargoyle vomits rainwater in disgust
Then, by some miracle or satanic curse
Freed from its frozen granite form
Stretches stone limbs, never used
Closes gaping mouth, favours narrow grin
Cruel and merciless
As it creeps with awkward, jerking movements
Down the holy façade
To lurk amongst tombstones below
Waiting, watching no longer with impotent gaze
Ready for the crowds to disgorge
Their rote motions completed, prayers mouthed
All without feeling nor with faith
Returning to the worldly world they own
The gargoyle is ready, prepares to leap
Bring vengeance, justice down upon them
Unheeding of pity, having never known it
Filled with righteous ire or hateful disgust
No longer observer, but instrument of destruction

THE GARGOYLICON : IMAGININGS AND IMAGES

GARGOYLES

Sherry Poff

Would we, if we could choose,
choose this face? These wings?
The cold sneer, calculated
to instill fear, halt advance?

Perched as we are, on places of worship,
learning, we would, if we could,
welcome the seeker, stranger.
But other hands formed the visage

set in stone, which he alone
could choose. He who wielded
the chisel, the hammer, worked
his own will on our faces.

But deep in darkness, our hollow eyes
invite your gaze, tender regard.
For our brothers walk among you
stony of face and afraid.

Well they understand their split lip,
misshapen nose, cannot reveal
what a look could show:
their longing to be known.

WHERE GARGOYLES REIGN

Patricia Hope

They are not as stone-faced
as you imagine, wait until the dark
of night to blink. They know their street,
who comes and who goes, who is late,
who is early, who picks the tourists'
pitiful pockets, when the bells toll, and for whom?

They are patient but not kind,
spewing dirty water on anything
and anybody they can, sometimes, with
small roof stones embedded in their vomit
of hatred for the two-legged creatures
that walk in and out of their line of vision.

They dream of all they'd do if they could walk,
never to squat again on this roof, but move around
and see beyond the edge of sight. How they
long to see what lies at their back
or over the rooftop across the street, to turn
the corner at the end of the block.

They curse their maker, argue
among themselves who can spit water the farthest,
and complain that no one looks up anymore.
Soon the sun will set. The moonless sky
will fill with stars and give them privacy. They plot
their escape, plan which humans below
                    should take their place.

Night Watch

Michelle Young

I shift center of gravity, adjust my grip —
chips of granite scales crack,
shed from dragon-shaped feet and toes
that end in curved, razored talons.
Debris falls unnoticed
into starless night, lands
in the quiet of empty sidewalk.

Centuries of molting disappears
on the wind, or blends with wet
rotting leaves to be washed away
during spring's heavy storms.
The magic that animates the gargoyle
renews my strength, repairs
my stiff, grotesque body
and sends me on a night watch.

My eyes melt yellow,
become brighter, hotter
until ruby embers flame,
releasing soul to sky.
I find the evil ones,
bring them nightmares,
torture souls until they beg
for death. This is the warning,
the gift of repentance I offer.
I will fulfill my duty until earth
is consumed in the final fire,
when I'll return home.

WRATH OF GARGOYLES

Scott J. Couturier

Guarding gates to fanes of divine guerdon,
gray wings outspread in menacing display:
immobilized by Time's immense burden
save when some sinner incites their dismay –

A demon's visage with mandibles bared,
imbued by mason's most blasphemous fears:
atop cathedral's spire its kind crouch laired,
arousing once yearly to reap arrears.

At Hallowmas twilight all skywards swarm,
tongues panting hot for unpenitent souls:
horrid stone wards hungry to inflict harm
'pon that frail flock they otherwise patrol.

Hewn by mortal hand in unhallowed guise
to serve Creator's will, more grotesque still:
swooping down by night on foolish & wise,
Hell's coffers with unclean spirits they fill.

Vengeance of a wicked & wrathful god –
spared neither claw & fang nor ire & rod.
Heretics by gargoyles brutally gnawed,
steeple sides dyed red in newly shed blood.

LITHOTROPH

From the Greek meaning 'rock eater'

John C. Mannone

They sentinel old college buildings
not like their ancestors who merely
gargled rain water, spit it out away
from building walls, though they still
haunt entrances to Catholic chapels
but Protestants have their own set
of demons in their pews and pulpits

just like the peculiar priests gathering
in the sacristies and graves, and groves
where some who worship Baal are loud
and drunk in orgies throughout the night.

At midnight, the winged dragontailed
devils, dark lion-bodied angels, monster
birds from hell roam the dim-lit halls
and university libraries, seeking whom
they may devour: fear-stricken students
in final exams week; insensitive faculty.

There's something about the savor
of blood, like good wine, when aged
in sin. Sometimes the chimera will
let them go—to live in consummate fear
to improve the taste of flesh for later.

Just before the dawn, when the evil
ones have sated themselves with humans,
they return to stone, eat into it, during day
they absorb the sun above disinterested
passersby until there's a dark opportunity
to morph from stone to gargoyle, crunch
tasty bone once again.

OLIVEGOYLE

Jay Sturner

Dear reader, how might the following story—or any of the thousands already told the world over of inanimate objects coming to life—be explained? I believe, that with the passing of centuries, a significant buildup of residual magic, misspoken curses, incomplete incantations, and other dark emissions has encircled the earth to such an extent that, by some strange, mysterious law of attraction, a number of curious objects—such as Gothic statues—have become enchanted. This is, of course, just a theory. Perhaps you've one of your own.

> Rock should not walk in the evening.
> — from "The Gods of the Mountain" by Lord Dunsany

Rain slants heavy like a torrent of curses from an angry god. The twin dragons of Altgeld Hall at Northern Illinois University crouch on either side of the front archway, spewing water from stone grins. In the nearby garden plot, a human-sized statue stands dreaming and alone. This is Olivegoyle; not a *true* gargoyle, but one of several grotesques stationed on and around the Gothic-style hall, a building often referred to as 'The Castle' for its turreted design. Today, sadness pours over Olivegoyle with the rain; not only is she alone in the garden—separated from the others due to past lightning strikes—she is headless. Recently her bat-like visage was stolen, and subsequently lost, by a drunken prankster. Often her consciousness thinks: *My head is gone, I must go get another.* But she cannot do much without eyes.

The storm retreats to the surrounding farmland; a million raindrops now echo across campus beneath an emergent moon. The dragon gargoyles wiggle and snarl, crack free of their stone foundations and launch themselves from their respective perches. Spiraling up and into the sky, they glide playfully across the moonlit rooftops. Next they chase each other into the cold, thin atmosphere at the edge of space. There they dance medieval jigs, growl long-forgotten laments, breathe imaginary fire. For a time they engage in mock aerial combat and swooping aerobatics, their eyes ablaze in a field of stars. Satisfied with their play, the dragons then return to The Castle. They sniff wildly about the garden, soon picking up the scent of Olivegoyle's prankster like a pair of bloodhounds. Not having far to go, they alight on the ledge of the man's dorm room window and scuttle through its billowing curtains.

As a new dawn swallows the last fragments of night, as fog lifts off lawns to swirl about the legs of walking students, a piercing scream shoots across campus, scattering pigeons from rooftop perches. At Altgeld Hall, a student has taken notice of Olive-goyle's *new head*. Rivulets of blood candy-stripe the stone body beneath. Several students gather at the statue, gasping and crying as they recognize the horror-stricken face of their peer, his sev-ered head now stuck atop the soiled grotesque. Blood pools inside the throat, rises, spurts intermittently from the gaping mouth. And then a wisp of steam—or perhaps an outward *sigh*—escapes into the brisk morning air.

The Watcher

Magnolia Silcox

There he sits on top of the church with his dead, cold eye
Sits there and watched the world go by
By night his fearsome face frightens evil away
Then he turns back to stone at the break of day
The people fear but respect him
He is their protector even though he looks like a demon
He flies around and devours evil creatures
He sits there watching over the spiritual welfare of old
religious preachers
His job was often a very thankless one
But with the support of his winged friends, he is sure to get the
job done

He is often feared
But by the townsfolk, he is respected and revered
At the sinful folks, he will roar and snarl
It causes their blood to boil and skin to curl
However, he is not a malevolent being
But he is sure to make sure they aren't sinning
He hears the people's prayers inside the holy place
Their cries to the saint's and Mary to stay in God's grace
But demonic spirits always stick to the people like parasites
Which leaves the poor gargoyle working long nights
These demons try to turn good people into sinful beings
Which the gargoyle hates the most of all wicked things
They will become evil due to these demonic entities
Changing their lifestyles and the very core of their identitie
He guards their pureness by gliding through the air
Stopping for a short period to watch and stare
Sometimes his adventures become rather chaotic
Seeing the dirty things people do at night makes him rather sick
They often hurt the innocent
And kill them for nothing more than a quick cent
They mock the gargoyle until they realize he is sentient
Little do they realize that he is a wise creature who is ancient
For he has been sculpted several years ago

The good architects have worked on him through the sun and snow
Some see him as nothing more than a decoration
While others see him as a means to maintain the church's holy
reputation
He has to admit that he is neither beautiful nor attractive
With a lions body and an eagle's face, somepeople find him
                                        quite psychoactive
But he's not meant to be a friendly beast
Turning all evil into a midnight's feast
He devours Satanic people engulfing them in flames
By the morning no one dares to even utter their names
He has become numb to the evil folk's ear-piercing screams
But yet he felt sorry for leaving children with nightmare fueled
                                        dreams
He is unfortunately not able to save everyone from Satan's evil lies
For the demons and Satan, himself often hide behind a friendly
                                        disguise
The devil fills their heads with promises of money and riches
Turning them into greedy civilians that rise up and create militias
They turn their back against their brothers
To gain power they go as far as to murder their own mothers
So many horrible things bring the gargoyle to tears
But as many bad things happen, he hears the good happening
                                        with his ears
For as many bad people, there are several more filled with goodwill
There are some humans that are charitable and helpful
He wishes he could thank those people that always help out
But during the day he is nothing more than a mere water spout
He sits in silence as thoughts swirl in his head
For he is the watcher over souls alive and dead
For during the day he is a mere spectator
However, during the night he is the people's defender

A Gargoyle's Meditations

Frank Coffman

I

I'm not a mere *grotesque* for decoration
Of this old church; I serve in functions four:
The first, that they, by my *misthought* creation
Would ward off Evil, keep the Devil from the door;
The second, I would frighten the congregation
Into believing the Horrors of Hell held more
Than could be shaped by their imagination;
Third, to lure pagans who might such a faith explore;
Fourth, through my gullet and frightening maw,
The torrents from the heavens would be spewed
Away from the masonry—and thus protect
Foundation stones. But those vomits from out my jaw,
Unbeknownst to them, keep my stone life renewed!
For centuries, thus, I've had time to reflect.

II

My fellows and I, whatever our shape or size,
Look down, beholding all the vile deeds of Man.
Yes, we have watched, through graven greyrock eyes,
Your wretched lives—much briefer than our span.
We've seen enough to do more than surmise
Your worldwide woes, each once-more-thwarted plan.
You think us fixed in place, but we have a surprise!
Though doomed to wait and watch—to move we can!

On nights when the sky is clear and the moon is new,
On All Hallow's Eve and on each pagan date—
Each Quarter of the World's Great Wheel—a few
Of us fly forth to *forage*, to investigate.
Shadow by shadow, we rarely come in view,
Those doomed who see us meet a grisly fate.

A Gargoyle's Meditations

Paul Mutartis Boswell

III
But most nights I sit here and I sometimes dream,
My eyes wide open, but there's a trance of rest
I can invoke. You folk who are sure we seem
Completely lifeless, that we could not be blessed
With any sentience: no power to laugh—or scream—
You are bemused. For we have powers unguessed
And a zest for Life; we too can plot and scheme
And roam when the Sun slips far below the West.

And like your ilk, we too can crave and lust.
I have stone dreams to revel and copulate
With *Sheela na gigs*, or to slay with talon thrust
Any of you who wander out too late.
It's right your pitiful kind returns to dust,
While we endure and watch—and more than wait!

First appeared in *Black Flames & Gleaming Shadows,*
Bold Venture Press, 2020: 39-40.

WILL I EVER FEEL THE RAINFOREST
ON MY SKIN?

Rebecca Thrush

How many passing particles cut into me
Like a never-ending barrage of insults?
They are so small that only their cumulative hurt
Registers along my rippled edges

Am I hurtling towards monumental mountains
Careless and hidden by my mirrored comrades?
Maybe these deflated days are just a side effect
Of being broken by an unseen wall

The stony exterior of my life is discolored
As years of moss and murk still grow
And as the edges transform into a hardened guardian
I feel your roots pulling me down by my toes

Has the wing-ed beast at your steps
Ever left the confines of this suburban pseudo-paradise?
Does he know that his life is forever resigned
To being a kitschy gimmick for trick-or-treaters?

They are always treated because you are too afraid
To try to trick and fail them, to fail yourself
Those children are passing through your parcel
And forgetting the impact as soon as they press send

The Dragon of Rouen

Maxwell I. Gold

There at the foot of gray steeples where the bodies of old winged creatures were amassed into a stone roost, the dragons of Rouen crowned sweet lavender nights. I felt a thousand lidless eyes watch me through the old Gaulish streets, surrounded by the solemnity of old grotesques, the ancient cathedrals lurched over the town as the head of the old gargoyle sneered from spire to spire.

Toothless and strange, the dragons trapped inside dogmatic castles kept the ire of crimson demons and ghouls at bay as they charged forth from mysterious lands cradled in the shadowy east across a vast, hungry sea. In the purple hills where dreams of old Norman kings were restless and green, still, the dragons of Rouen kept steadfast as I watched them leer into the night, waiting for what was to come, always vigilant, those eternal sentinels of dust and rock.

GARGOYLE THOUGHTS

Frank Coffman

I am not formed as these who walk below,
But formed *by* them who have much quicker brains.
They can't imagine that I could observe—*or know!*
They find me interesting, but useful only when rains
Are gathered and spewed from my grim, malformed maw.
To believe *I think* breaks every natural law
They hold as "Truth." Though my cold, hollow heart
Will never feel their kind's hot coursing blood,
Yet still I know my folk and play a part—
To weather all weathers, bright day or snow or flood.
The calm, dry days they love bring me the pain
Of thirst. But, ever patient, I pray for rain.
Though slow of wit, at least I know my purpose.
Many who move below me settle for less.

GRIMLORD

Harris Coverley

He stands at the bottom of the pit
    He has little else now but the pit

We come to the edge
And look down in the dim light of the sun
    Creaking nervously through the gaps in the dome above
    us

He is as solid and as grey as the day he died
    Unreachable as always
Two hundred feet deep
Trapped between the cyclopean walls
    The Creator of All but a mere misplaced gargoyle
Thin streams of murky water dripping onto his green shoulders

And we float down our rose petals
    And carved wooden offerings
To join the earthen mass about his feet
    Rotting into a black soil in which nothing will ever grow

We know fully that he is dead
    We know fully that he has gone for good
But we carry on still the rituals of our fathers
    And our grandfathers's grandfathers

The dust rises
    And stays in the air
        An eldritch glow about his body

His great arms held aloft in agony
His mouth open to call his people to him
Now frozen for eternity
      Or until the sun grows yet colder
           And our world breaks into nothing

WE SNARL ALONE

Leslie Soule

We snarl alone, Rosita and I –
Fixed in place as we've been
Now, for centuries
It starts somewhere deep in the gullet
Rumbles in the stone pot of the stomach
Erupts through sharp teeth
We shiver in the cold, wings unfurled
We bake in the heat, claws extended
We watch the pilgrims below, on their holy journeys
Roger took a dive the other day,
And killed a man
Rosita and I, remain
We Snarl Alone.

Masquers

Kyla Lee Ward

GARGOYLES, AS THEY GRUMBLE

Kyla Lee Ward

Sydney, 1858

nastystupidfeathers
sillysmoothcheeks
handsnotclawed
nofangs
curls

It is a blistering afternoon at the work site, trapped under heavy, grey-white clouds. Heat presses down upon the stretch of churned clay and bleached, blonde grass that will become the University of Sydney, as though trying to drive the arches and buttresses back down into the earth. Architect Edmund Blackett favours the style of the gothic revival and thus there are gargoyles laid out in a row, next to a fine, large angel and a cluster of carven terminals for the beams of the Great Hall. All are destined to trim the roof, both inside and out, but their installation is still some weeks away.

The gargoyles, exquisitely fashioned though they are of buttery Pyrmont yellow block, are disgruntled. Their ribbed horns curve, carved by master masons; their paws and webbed toes clutch at their pediments. Today there are visitors at the site wearing polished leather boots and fitted trousers, slippers and hooped skirts. Being set upon dirt at the foot of walls you were made to surmount would put anyone out of sorts and, of course, the proximity of human feet is an insult to anything with wings. But added to this, what do the visitors gaze upon and to what do they deliver their compliments? The angel.

The photographer's apprentice raises the pan.
Flash!

In that moment—the moment when he should have beheld his angel bathed in splendour—Edmund Blackett glances inadvertently towards the gargoyles. Scoured white and black by the burning magnesium, the after-image shows him blinking orbs and flexing claws, the slight flaring of stone nostrils. The stretching of bat-like wings.

nastystupidfeathers

Blackett blinks, his eyes watering.

"You shouldn't leave out the gargoyles."

The voice at his elbow sends Blackett spinning, nearly costs him his topper. Despite the heat (which in Sydney, in this season, heralds a storm), he is dressed for the visiting dignitaries in frock coat and starched collar. The mason, on the other hand, is garbed in loose white. His hat is broad, his whiskers voluminous. He fixes Blackett with eyes like blue beads, saying, "They won't settle."

Blackett glances across the work site, at the wilting parliamentarians, old grammarians and their wives all hastening towards the refreshment tent, then back down at the mason. "What did you say?"

"Begging your pardon, Mr Blackett, but they won't."

Belatedly, Blackett remembers the man's name. "What do you mean, Popplewell? The foundations are settling? Lord have mercy, we're never seeing cracks?"

"Indeed no, Mr Blackett. It's the gargoyles."

This, thinks Blackett, is beyond any kind of response—for obviously he did *not* see the wings stretch, the nostrils flare, nor truly hear that stony grumble. It was all a trick of the heat and shimmering, cloud-filtered light. The only dignified option is for him to walk away and yet, he may not follow the oh-so gentlefolk (who applauded very nicely at his speech). He must still give instructions, turn his men to their tasks and secure the site against the oncoming deluge. The Angel of Knowledge and its shield-bearing brethren must be tarped.

So hot it is and yet so still. Not even a breath of wind. The cry of crickets in the grass grinds against his skull.

"All I'm saying," Popplewell continues, "Is that you spoke all about the angels, how the big one means we come to learning through Christ and the little ones—very nice carving from young James there—are all the different faculties as make up the university. But nothing about the meaning of the gargoyles."

The Angel of Knowledge is yellow block but the others are all of pristine jarrah wood, for attaching to the beams. Twelve stiff-backed angels carrying twelve shields, each bearing a symbol of their faculty. Blackett appreciates the relevance of an abacus to Arithmatic and a star to Astronomy. But a frog-like face of yellow block, eyes bulging and mouth gaping wide? Barnett finally finds his voice. "They don't mean anything."

"Again, your pardon, Sir. But they do."

Another flash, but this comes from the celestial pan, charged with divine powder over mere magnesium. An almighty rumble banishes the crickets and rolls over the whole, charged scene—in the distance, the smokey blur of Sydney town, the nearer spectacle of oxen hauling carts of stone up the hill. Nearer still, his assistant Colby mops his face with a kerchief. The photographer's apprentice—a young lad in knee breeches and a flat cap—stands gaping at Popplewell, rather than folding his master's equipment into its cherrywood box. The refreshment tent billows in a sudden gust of wind, canvas straining like a sail against the ropes, and Blackett is released.

"Colby!" he calls, "Colby, I need the tarpaulins brought out and secured over the woodwork. Don't forget the window sills."

"Right you are, Sir!" The burly Colby, a mason like Popplewell but blissfully free from fancy, tips his hat as he strides down the hill, rousing the men into action. Blackett hastens towards the tent, to check that the ropes are secure.

In Blackett's wake, the photographer's apprentice stares at the gargoyles. Uncle John has long since repaired to the tent, sipping tea and hunting unctiously for commissions. The stone creatures fascinate whereas the angel does not. With its impossibly perfect hair, its blind, stone eyes and hand raised in benediction, it is just another condescending man, raised by birth to the bench or the pulpit. She has seen more than enough of those.

"Afternoon, Miss," says Popplewell.

She stands firm, for she breaks no law in assisting her uncle or wearing the clothes most suitable to the task. Her sex is no secret, although neither is it something they feel the need to broadcast. "Afternoon," she bids him back.

Behind her, the hood of the camera lifts and fills, lifts and fills, as waves of dust are blown across the work site. At the edge of the trampled track, the blonde grass bends almost to the earth. The oxen bellow. Soon the cloud pall will split and all the yellow fins, the flaring ears, the nostrils and tusked mouths will darken and run with water. But this is a gargoyle's function—they do not fear it. Still they stand together, photographer and mason, until at long last, she turns to him. "What do the gargoyles mean?"

#

Inside the tent, it is stuffy and as hot as out; moreover, an inordinate number of crickets seem also to have taken shelter. The tea, as dispensed, is lukewarm. Blackett stands with his back to the rattling flap, a china cup in hand, smiling at the university's benefactors (most of whom would rather erect a wooden shed than a masterpiece for the ages, and then attempt to sell it off as warehouse space).

"But look here, Blackett." A florid face accosts him, all judicial brow and jowls. Fleetingly, he imagines how the man would look as a gargoyle, immortalised in stone but not in the way he would doubtless prefer. "Do we in truth need all this decoration, these carvings and things?"

"It's traditional for university buildings," he replies, "as for churches built in the gothic style."

"Tradition is all very well," The new speaker is, he believes, the Member for Northumberland. "But I can't see how it benefits us. We're a business community. We live by our exports, not our speculations."

"Young men reading their Homer and Petrach," His Honour pontificates, "don't need to be distracted from their study by all these frills. And that, Sir, is a *proper* education."

The Member smiles. "And down at the Rocks they can read their Ovid." A burst of laughter from the men—the ladies present look to hems befouled by crossing the paddock. The Anglican Bishop of Sydney responds that he, himself, has no objection to the angels but feels that even in churches, gargoyles are as unnecessary as Ovid to a Christian curriculum. "Nonsense, your Grace," responds the Member. "Where would we be if the devil spoke no Latin?"

Blackett sips his tea, remembering his Vitruvius. In any building, harmony must be preserved at all cost. He feels the tent shaking around him and his architect's instinctive awareness flies to the building, as though the same resonance pervades the heavy beams and solid, interlocking blocks. Without their glass, the arching windows are as yet so delicate.

But now the Governor's wife approaches.

"Well, I for one adore your angel," says the dowager, peering at him through dust-spotted spectacles. "And I found your speech most affecting. As you said, today, we lay the foundations of our country's future."

"That angel," he responds, "Will watch over us for the next three hundred years."

#

"The *other* knowledge?" says the apprentice.

Popplewell nods. "Such as they in the tent don't wish to know and would keep from such as us. Such things as we mostly learn anyway."

The gargoyles loom expectantly, as she considers this proposition. It is hard to loom at the level of feet, but they manage. It is true that most admiration as gargoyles receive comes from people who allow their gaze to wander out of windows and up drainpipes, their ears to track the faintest of gurgles, over lessons. Who seek out masons marks, pondering what lies above and below, all the while concealing their own grotesqueness from the world. But such recognition is not enough. When their own architect dismisses them, it can never be enough.

Nonetheless, John's niece will do what she can. She nods courteously to the mason, then charges the flash pan. She has long since worked out how to operate the camera single-handed.

#

Flash!

The walls of the tent turn white. But for so long as Blackett pauses, cup halfway to his lips, there is no rumble of thunder. Only a guttural gurgling, that can only mean the rain has come.

nastystupidhomer
sillydullpetrach
curlysmoothangels
we wait
till
dark

#

Sydney, 1888

"Excuse me, Sir, but what is that piece back there?"

Archibald Liversidge, Dean of the newly minted Faculty of Science, gazes upon his student. The presence of the young lady, in her severe blouse and blue serge skirt, and the faculty itself are both largely his achievements.

"That?" He reaches past the geodes and fossils, to the uneven lump of sandstone at the back. A roughly shaped grey lump, perhaps the size of a head: he draws it forward on the bench, so she may examine it. She leans closer, her expression intent.

The arguments there had been, against admitting female students! On his side there was science. On the other, endless bleating about the impropriety of having both sexes present during a lecture on classics, lest Ovid make his way into the discourse.

"It was a sculpture," says the object of their concerns. She is quiet in class but observant, oh yes. The first to ask this question all year and one of only few. "Badly eroded, yet not by water, I think. The surface is too rough."

"Yes, that is perhaps the most curious feature." With a flat palm, Liversidge brushes the vestigial curls. His own are thinning. "Thirty years ago, when it first opened, there was an angel statue atop the Great Hall."

"Thirty years?" She glances askance at the head.

"It only stood for twenty. Have you seen the photos on the wall of the admissions office?"

The air is sultry today, typical of a Sydney summer. The geology lab is cool but through the tracery of the window, heat presses down on a quadrangle of bleached and beaten grass.

The student shakes her head and then her brow furrows. "What was the statue made of?"

"Ah now, that's the thing. So far as I was able to determine, exactly the same stone as the other ornamentation on the facade."

The furrow deepens, for as they both know, the gargoyles and trefoils, the crockets on the clock tower, are all still in excellent condition. "There must have been some unique factor."

"What would you suggest?"

"The position, sticking up like a needle with no shelter from the rain," she offers. "Or perhaps a corrosive effect from the metal of its mount."

"Both excellent answers." Liversidge beams. A sound like a gurgling chuckle comes from somewhere close by – perhaps in the quadrangle, though through the window, nothing can be seen save a boy in cricket whites hastening in from the lower field. He should be in class already. "I myself suspect it was struck by lightning."

"That might explain the unusual surface."

"Yes," Liversridge replies, "It almost looks like it was eaten."

Another chuckle, like water running down a drainpipe. The student crosses to the window and peers over the lawn. Then, for no apparent reason, she looks up.

"You should go look at the photos," says Liversidge. "There is an absolutely charming one of an old mason, standing next to the gargoyles, before they were installed."

"The gargoyles!" The girl exclaims, face lighting up as though from a camera flash. "All those mouths!"

Believing she speaks merely of the sound, Liversidge frowns. "But there's been no rain for weeks."

"There will be, " she says. "A storm is coming."

The Gargoyle Watches the Rains End

Amelia Gorman

not a thousand times like before, but once
...and slowly. how long until stone-on-stone

glass in his throat, a rasp, a strange friction
how he cracks when the field, cracks. cracks

when the hot winds blow, the red clouds gather
in bloom over a girl gathering dead lavender

below. oh for the drink he'd take if he'd known
the last rains were the last, oh for the spit

he'd loose. what good are his flippered fingers now
or his big O of a mouth? what good his short tapers

inside that spout, or the long neck that stretches
out to look at the girl and her basket and her thirst

in the dust of a sun going down? their thick tongues
missing water or wine, their afflictions tandem,

grapes crack on the vine. the iron bell echoes
like a thousand times before, and a dry moon rises.

Esme's Worst Nightmare

Wendy Harrison

"What in the name of all that's holy is that?" My husband's broad grin wavered.

"What does it look like?"

I chose my words carefully. "Grounds for divorce?"

We both stared down at the thing he had wheeled off the pickup ramp. I thought I had found a way to cope with his bringing home strange objects. Stay calm. Reason with him. Pick my battles. As a professor of world history, he had travelled to almost every continent, lecturing, researching, and worst of all, collecting. But when he was made head of the department, his administrative responsibilities occupied so much time, he let the younger faculty take up the travel slack. I was lulled into a false sense of freedom from the invasion into my home by the ugly and grotesque, like the voodoo doll from New Orleans. Victor thought the deal clincher with me would be that it came in its own coffin. Seriously.

The stone critter was around three feet tall. Its massive head had the ears of a cat, the wrinkles of a Shar Pei, an enormous nose and large fangs. It crouched on two legs which ended in clawed feet. Veined wings sprouted from its back. It was very old with multiple cracks in its surfaces.

"Isn't it great?" Victor's 52-year-old face, still handsome under silver hair, looked at me with the hope for a miracle of a ten year old bringing home a stray puppy.

I was speechless for a moment. "It's a gargoyle. A frigging gargoyle."

"I know. Hard to believe it was just sitting there, at the dump."

This was so typical. My husband went to the town landfill to drop off our trash and brought back the scariest thing I'd ever seen. I fell back on my coping plan. After a deep, calming breath, I said, "You need to take it back." As he opened his mouth to respond, I stopped him. "This one isn't negotiable. I won't have this here. We have no room for it, and it's the ugliest thing I've ever seen." He started to respond, but I stopped him. "No. You've crossed the line this time."

We'd been married long enough for him to know he had no wiggle room. My face was as stony as the creature's.

"All right. But he'll have to stay until I can get some help moving him."

"Him?"

He nodded. "Fang."

Oh my god. He had already given it a name. But I was unmoved. "How did you get it on the truck?"

He looked down at the creature. He was stalling. This wasn't going to be something I'd want to hear. "Three guys helped me."

A high-pitched wail startled me. I looked down and saw Gabby, our calico cat, at my feet, back arched, tail straight up in the air. She must have followed me outside. I bent and lifted her rigid body. Comforting her, I stroked her back. "It's all right, sweetheart. The bad Fang won't hurt you. I promise." I glared at Victor. "You have 48 hours to get this thing out of here. I'm not kidding."

As I carried Gabby back to the house, I felt the creature's eyes following me. When I looked back at him, I was sure he was drooling. Forty-eight hours couldn't go quickly enough.

The next morning, after a restless night, I dressed and went to the kitchen to feed Gabby. She usually ran to greet me as I walked toward the cat food cabinet, but she didn't show up, even at the sound of the flip-top can opening.

I wandered through the house, calling her, and then opened the front door, thinking she might have gotten loose somehow. I had almost forgotten our unwelcome visitor. Fang sat on the lawn next to the driveway where Victor had left him. I shook off the fear I felt at its lurking presence. It was a block of stone. That's all. I continued my search for Gabby but finally gave up. She had gotten loose before, but she always came home when she got hungry.

Victor appeared in the hallway as I stepped back inside. I asked, "Have you seen Gabby?"

He shook his head. "Did she get out again?"

"I guess so, but I have to leave. I have a showing this morning for the Astor house." As a real estate agent, getting the listing for this grand house was a coup. I grabbed my purse, and Victor and I left together. When we passed Fang, Victor patted his head. I shuddered but restrained myself from reminding my exasperating husband that the clock was ticking.

He read my mind. Victor, that is. Not Fang, even though I still could feel his eyes on me. "I'll take care of it today. I'm sure I can get some of the students to help. Maybe one of them would even like to keep him. Fang will be gone by tomorrow. I promise."

"Maybe we shouldn't talk about this in front of him." I was only half joking. Those eyes.

We exchanged our usual goodbye kiss and left at the same time, leaving Fang alone to contemplate his future back at the dump.

The house showing went well, and I was getting back in my car when my cellphone rang. I didn't recognize the number, but I was used to having strangers call to talk about the listings I had.

"Is this Ms. Miller?" When I said yes, the voice continued. "Is your husband Victor Miller?" I turned to ice. I had never known what that would feel like. "There's been an accident. He's here at Boston Hospital."

"Is he all right?" It felt like a stupid question. If he were all right, it would be his voice on the phone.

"He's being taken to surgery. If you can, I think you should come." She told me what floor he was on and I hung up.

The trip into the city felt like it was taking forever, but in half an hour I was pulling into the parking garage. I ran to the hospital entrance and took the elevator to the fourth floor. A nurse told me where I could wait until a doctor could talk to me. I asked if she knew what had happened. "All I know is that it was a single-car accident on Pine Street." That was the road Victor took to go from our house to the university. It wasn't heavily travelled. How was this possible?

It was an hour before a woman in scrubs came to find me. I stood. "How is he?"

She gestured for me to sit. "His truck drove off the road and hit a tree. He had multiple fractures and a head injury. We've repaired the bone damage but…." Her hand touched my arm, and I held my breath. "We've placed him in a medically induced coma to allow his brain swelling to go down."

"How could this have happened? He's the most cautious driver I know."

She shook her head. "You might be able to get more information from the police. That's all I know at this point. I'm afraid he can't have visitors right now. I promise if there's any change, you'll be called. Do you have anyone who can keep you company? It could be days before we know where we are."

Was there anyone I wanted to be with? I couldn't think of anyone but Victor. "I'll be all right. But please, call any time, no matter when it is."

On the way home, I drove the length of Pine Street. It wasn't hard to see where the accident happened. Crime scene tape fluttered around a large old oak tree with a deep crack in the side facing the road. The pickup had already been towed away, but there was broken glass on the ground. Skid marks had left ridges in the grass between the road and the tree. It looked like Victor had tried to stop. Why didn't it respond?

When I got home, I parked on the street. As I walked past Fang, I felt a chill. I tried not to look at him but couldn't stop myself. He was staring back at me, with hunger in his eyes. I told myself I was just upset and imagining things and went inside, locking the door behind me.

My first call was to the Dean of Victor's department. I explained what happened, and he offered whatever help I might need. Victor was a star at the school, and his research had attracted the best students and a lot of grant money. I was sure the Dean's concern was genuine but at least a little selfish.

My next call was to the police. The woman on the phone said the detective wasn't there but she would let him know I called. She did give me the name and number of the towing company.

A man answered and confirmed they had Victor's pickup. I could come to look at it, although he warned me it would be upsetting to see.

After checking around the house for Gabby with no success, I walked past Fang without looking at him. The drive to the towing place took me past the accident scene again, and I tried not to look at that either.

The lot was surrounded by a chain-link fence. I walked through an open gate to a large garage and called out. A man in greasy jeans came from the back, his name written in script on his shirt. "George?" I asked. "I'm Esme Miller. I called about seeing my husband's truck."

"The accident on Pine Street?" I nodded. "I just got done going over it. The cops asked me to check it out."

I remembered what I had seen at the accident location. "Why didn't his brakes work?"

His muscled shoulders shrugged. "No reason I could find. Even with the damage from the tree, the brakes seemed to be working."

"I want to see the truck."

His reluctance was clear, but I insisted. I followed him to the fenced yard where wrecked vehicles littered the area. Victor's was at the front. I tried to forget my beautiful husband had been inside the mass of mangled metal. The front of the car was accordioned into the driver's seat. I looked for a deflated airbag and, when I didn't see it, I asked George what happened to it.

"It didn't open." Before I could ask, he added, "It should've worked. I don't know what to tell you."

I left with more questions than I had before. Nothing made sense. When I got home, I was exhausted. I wasn't someone who took afternoon naps, but I couldn't keep my eyes open. I went upstairs and pulled back the log cabin quilt I had made when we were first married. Sobs overcame me, and I cried until I had no more tears. I wasn't the praying kind, but I begged for Victor's recovery, hoping someone or something would take pity on me.

Part of me was aware I was sleeping, but it wasn't enough to drive away the nightmare that engulfed me. I was sitting in the living room with Gabby on my lap and Victor next to me, holding my hand. We were watching the original "Hunchback of Notre Dame." Charles Laughton appeared on the top of the church, his deformed shape in black and white in shadow as he talked to Esmeralda, his unrequited love. One of the gargoyles decorating the buttresses of the building sprang to life. I watched in horror as the gargoyle threw Quasimodo off the roof and pulled Esmeralda to him.

My screams woke me. I gasped for breath as I looked around the room. It was calm and quiet, but the tangled quilt was evidence of my terrifying dream. When I looked toward the windows, I realized it was dark out. I had slept away most of the afternoon. When I checked my phone, I saw a number of texts from friends of Victor at the university but no calls or texts from the hospital. I called anyway, and the operator told me his condition was stable but unchanged.

I wasn't hungry but knew I had to eat something if I was going to get through this. In the kitchen, I scrambled a couple of eggs and toasted a slice of bread. As I sat at the island, the house was quiet. Too quiet. I jumped at every sound. It was a relief when I was able to identify the rustling of leaves and the occasional car passing.

Rage overcame my pain. I had to do something about Fang. The image of the gargoyle pulling the screaming Esmeralda to his body felt like an omen. Maybe I was losing my mind, but I didn't care.

I went into the garage through the door from the kitchen. Victor had converted it into a workshop where he worked on restoring the old objects he had brought home over the years. Our cars usually sat in the driveway so he would have space to make as much of a mess as he wanted.

All the tools were hanging from pegboard Victor had installed on the walls. I walked around, looking for something I could use. There were several large sledge hammers Victor had bought to take out a concrete path that needed to be replaced two years ago. I had helped and been surprised by how much I enjoyed the physical act of destruction.

I pressed the button to open the garage door and hoisted one of the sledge hammers over my shoulder. I could sense Fang's awareness of my approach, which terrified me, but I couldn't stop now. I stood behind him where I could avoid his eyes. As I lifted the tool, I felt a force in the air, working against me, but I slammed the hammer down on the top of his head. It caught one of his ears, which broke off. I followed with the other ear and then forced myself to walk around to face him. Hatred poured off him, but my next blow caught the side of his neck. One of the cracks in the stone broke apart, and his head tumbled to the ground. I ran to where it landed and hammered it into a pile of formless stones.

After resting for a moment, I shoveled the pieces into a wheelbarrow and pushed it around to the backyard. There was a stand of trees at the back of our property, and that's where I buried the remains of Fang's head. "Please rest in peace," I murmured before turning to go back to where I had left the rest of him. The headless winged body was no longer threatening. I would deal with it later. At the moment, I desperately needed a drink.

As I started for the front door, I heard a plaintive "Meow." Gabby ran past and waited for me to open the door. We walked into the kitchen together, and I put down fresh food and water for her.

"Welcome home, little one." I stroked her as she ate. I took her presence as a sign Fang was truly gone. When my cellphone rang a few minutes later, I knew what I would hear.

"Ms. Miller? I have good news for you."

GRYPHONS
Ann Thornfield-Long

and grotesques
crouch in the corners
of gothic cathedrals

their dragon backs
arched, haunched
on pelves.

Scaly legs,
toenails grip the stone
from which they sprout.

Carved and twisted
tongues loll waiting
for the colonics

of rainy days.
Nothing stays
not even leaves,

they heave, gag,
wretch and spew
gastric juices

on multitudes
below who look
up to view

their faces. Observers
get what they deserve
gawking at misshapen

forms, ill-mannered
louts who stare
at bulging eye

and eagle beak.
Nothing matches
save the human

desire of height
to spit on those
less fortunate.

WHEN THE LEONIDS COME

David M. Hoenig

November 3, 1929

IT was a beautiful autumn night in New York, cool and crisp, and I walked the downtown streets in my Burberry trench coat. The smells of roasting chestnuts on street corners reminded me of the old country, though the absence of snow on the ground and ice in the air made me miss the simple days of sauna, cross-country skiing in the woods, and shared aquavit while looking at the cold stars of the night sky over Sweden.

And then I remembered other things—*things!*—from my long ago Sweden and shuddered. I knew better than to dwell on such, but memory is a strange and sorcerous beast, summoned by association and likely to rampage out of all control if not ruthlessly suppressed. Even so, the chill air and the stars high above in their recognisable constellations forced my thoughts to a particular autumn night with fresh snow on the ground and the celestial heavens reflected in the yet-unfrozen Vätttern lake, and what followed when I'd stared at the sight for too long.

And then of the bargain a much younger self had agreed to for fear of death.

A sudden, familiar nausea churned my bowels as sharp-edged memories a thousand years old threatened, and sour, acidic saliva flooded my mouth. I spat it out to the cobbled streets of this foreign city.

Commotion several streets away distracted me from the past. I consulted my pocket watch. *Soon,* I thought, with a quick glance at the stars overhead. I walked unhurriedly forward, and came to the edge of a frantic crowd, all looking up.

I heard a female voice. "Good God! Not even a week since Black Tuesday and it's another one!"

"He might as well do it, he's one of those responsible, am I right?" responded a man beside her. Other fragments of conversation and exclamations slid past.

High above, perhaps twenty or more stories, was a figure on a ledge at a building corner. He leaned forward, his arms behind him clutching at the stone bulwark there. I moved to a policeman who was just finishing ushering some people out of the street to a nearby sidewalk.

"Excuse me." When he turned, I proffered my business card to him. It read, simply: *Gustav Ahlberg, Eldritch Investigations.*

He took it and read. "We've got a situation here, Mr Ahlberg. What can I do for you?" He did a double-take at the card. "What's this 'Eldritch' baloney mean? You a private eye or something?"

"Something." I smiled reassuringly at him. "But in all seriousness, I'd be happy to go speak with that unfortunate man, see if I can help in some way."

"Why bother? Not like we can stop him if he wants to do it, and he ain't the first stockbroker—hell, not even the tenth—to want to splat himself these days. I'm just here to keep people back so they don't get hurt when he dives."

"Perhaps the stars will turn out to be just right for the poor gentleman, if that's even what he is—a bit hard to tell from down here, isn't it?"

"Are you nuts, buster?" He waved a hand scornfully. "It's definitely another jumper. Well, knock yourself out, just don't expect anything." He then scrawled something on a pad of paper in a small leather folio he carried, tore off the sheet, and handed it to me. "Show them this and they'll let you through."

It was a short walk to the building, and the policeman there read my note. "So you know, the elevator's out, mister."

"I don't mind the constitutional. May I go up?"

The officer went back to looking up as he waved me in, so I went.

The lobby was dark, and the door to the stairs was behind the bank of lifts. The climb up the stairs was indeed long, but as I went, I felt energised by it rather than fatigued. I consulted my pocket watch several times along the way but didn't have to adjust my pace at all. I marvelled at the gifts afforded me be those choices I'd made so long ago, even as I skirted the memories themselves most carefully. The opportunity to think led me to a statement attributed to a politician of the state of Massachusetts nearly eighty years prior, and which resonated for me as few others had in my unnaturally long life: 'Men, in a word, must necessarily be controlled, either by a power within them, or by a power without them; either by the Word of God, or by the strong arm of man; either by the Bible, or by the bayonet.' *Robert Charles Winthrop saw the truth so clearly*, I thought. *He would have made a good servant of the god had the right introductions been made. Who might have guessed that after less than a century of nationhood these Americans would have such clarity about the reality of existence?*

When I reached the uppermost floor, I found myself in a dark hallway. Ahead and to my left was a door which showed light through the gap between it and the floor. I went to it, through it, and was soon at the window closest to the distraught man. I went to it, and leaned out to see him holding onto the parapet above his head with both hands, several feet away. "Please sir, might I have a word with you?" I said as calmly as I could manage.

He started violently at my words. The wind whipped around us like something alive and violent, and he looked at me with wide, frantic eyes. "You try to stop me, I'm letting go!"

"I don't want to stop you, sir. In fact, if you intend to jump I would be happy to sanctify your death in the name of the god."

He blinked at me in disbelief. "Wha…?"

I kept my tone conversational as I interrupted him. "On the other hand, there are alternatives to death, if you are willing to explore them."

"What are you talking about?" He shifted his feet, trying to maintain purchase on the tiny ledge. "You're crazy!"

"That is the second time tonight I've been accused of insanity—you Americans seem to toss that phrase around far more casually than it deserves." I made eye contact with him and spoke to him in a low voice which held complete assurance. "Sir: I can assure you that the god *is*, in fact, listening tonight. What if I told you that this black time for you and your country will be but a distant memory in the very near future?"

"I've lost everything in the 'Crash', don't you get it? I'm ruined, there's nothing for me or my family but an insurance payout!" He looked desperately below him as he shifted his feet, and I saw that he meant to jump.

I kept my voice even, my tone sure, even as the wind whipped fiercely around us. "Oh, there is more, much more for you and your loved ones, my dear sir, and your life is worth many times more than a negligible insurance payout. You see, I can offer you peaceful rest throughout this challenging and perilous time and ensure that your family would receive the money your death would earn them. In addition, I can offer you a future you will awaken to in which the money lost in the past week will be but a drop of unconcern."

He looked at me incredulously. "You can seriously make all that happen?"

I felt the beginning of a smile pull at the corner of my mouth. "And more."

He looked down, and I saw him weighing things before he looked back at me. I brought my right hand from my pocket. "Look into this mirror, friend, and all I've offered will be yours." I tilted it upwards for him, so that when he'd look, he would see the reflected heavens above.

I kept my gaze on him to avoid looking in the glass myself, and our eyes met, held, and then he looked into the mirror. "Oh. Oh my," he said.

I could see the reflection of shooting stars at which he stared echoed in his eyes, and then he shrieked as the god I served entered him. He writhed, face twisted in a rictus of horror as he screamed, and I saw the exact moment when he turned to granite and there was only the sound of the wind. I waited, my hand outstretched as the heavens returned to their cold quiescence.

A different voice then issued from the man's mouth, as though from a throat made of crushed stone. "You've done well, minion."

A dangerous feeling of pride rose in me, but I squashed it down in order to answer humbly. "The Leonids' conjunction is upon us again, Master."

"I am close, but not yet close enough to manifest fully. My time is still not at hand."

"How long must I wait, Master?"

"As long as it takes! I will arrive in My full power only when the celestial alignment favours My ascendance."

I shivered, but not from the cutting wind.

"Plant more such seeds, minion."

I bowed my head in acquiescence before speaking. "Give me the power, Master, and I will prepare them—as this one—for your coming, that they may be awakened to serve You."

"Yes. And take care you do not fail Me—your centuries of service are not yet done." There was a final grating sound and the gravelly throat fell silent.

I raised my head then to see a statue at the ledge of the building: the man's face distorted in a grimace, clutching the cornerstone of the building just below the roof. I spat sour saliva to the gusty winds around us, leaned back into the room and closed the window behind me. I returned to the streets with a spring in my step, passing through the crowd still staring upwards, pointing and speaking together.

As I was walked away from the building, I felt a tap on my shoulder and turned to see the same policeman who'd given me the pass in the first place. "Well? Is the palooka going to jump or what? We ain't got all day, after all."

It was so easy to mislead the unwary when they wanted to be misled. "I'm afraid it was all a case of mistaken identity, Officer. It turned out to be nothing more than a gargoyle at the roofline."

"But we all saw it moving!"

I chuckled. "An amazing optical illusion! A scarf was caught about its neck giving it the appearance of a living man. You can certainly check it yourself, assuming the wind has not driven it from that perch—I had a rather good laugh when I'd finally huffed and puffed my way all the way up to it."

He turned to look, and I simply walked away. *Manhattan could use a few more gargoyles,* I thought as I looked at the tall buildings around me. I couldn't keep the smile off my face as I turned north onto Broadway as more meteors flashed overhead.

"Men, in a word, must necessarily be controlled, either by a power within them, or by a power without them," I murmured aloud. *I made my choice long ago to be controlled by the power within. I think I've gotten the best of that bargain so far.*

I wondered just how many gargoyles this city might hold in a hundred years or so, when the god's time of ascendance finally arrived. It made me both shudder and chuckle as I went uptown in this strange, new city under the same old—*very old!*—stars.

Apotropaia

Liam Hogan

When Professor Woodcock descended uninvited on the starship designers, advising them to incorporate grotesques into their state of the art, built in orbit, colossal super structure, they scoffed at him. And then they humoured him, asking whether he meant gargoyles?

The professor of medieval history, tweed clad, white haired, and bespectacled, frowned owlishly. "They're both apotropaia: guards against misfortune. But gargoyles are throated grotesques. Waterspouts, guiding rain away from masonry, protection from the elements. There's no rain, in space? Or are you ejecting other material?"

The engineers laughed and shook their heads at his superstitious nonsense. Though a couple of them did nudge one another. The colony ship Odyssey 1 was a closed ecosphere, with its own carbon cycle and water purification systems. Everything that could be reused, would be reused, over and over through the many generations it would take to get anywhere. But the one thing they didn't want—couldn't afford to keep—was the radioactive waste from the fusion reactors. There wasn't a lot of it, it being fusion. Lithium cladding mostly, stripped of valuable tritium. While considerable effort had been devoted to trying to use it as a propulsion material, the current thinking was it was best to simply eject it, to avoid contaminating the ion thrusters.

The waste had to be dispatched at a safe distance from the spaceship. And it had to be made to drift away from the hull—the last thing the colonists wanted, as they decelerated at the end of their one thousand year journey, was to run smack-bang into all the junk they'd kicked out along the way. Nano-scale particles for sure; but particles travelling at millions of kilometres an hour, and still radioactive.

So while grotesques were, everyone agreed, pointless, there was no reason they couldn't have some fun with their high-tech version of gargoyles, or "fusion reactor ejecta guide tubes", as they were officially designated. Monsters to police the boundaries of understanding. Portents of the overlap of the human and the divine, between sacred and profane, between heaven and earth. Between art, and science. A visual representation of the liminal: 3D printed monstrosities, long and thin—serpents, and wyrms, and things with no name, conjured from the printers' imaginations. Most of them wore the recognisable faces of the designers and even, as an afterthought and as a tribute, that of Professor Woodcock, peering at the cosmos through bottle thick spectacles.

He could have warned them about that. Could have told them about the sacrifices churches and cathedrals have always made to keep chaotic spirits at bay. The graven images of the priests and stonemasons, forever staring outward, ready and waiting to trap or frighten demons.

As the spaceship kicked out from Earth, the sun dwindling to just another bright star, those left behind—the engineers, scientists, and even Professor Woodcock—became dispirited and listless, wasting away as though cursed, as the thread connecting their bodies and their effigies thinned and frayed.

When the spaceship was a mere billion miles away, long before the Odyssey left the solar system, the stretched threads unravelled completely, and the clever men and women who had unwittingly enslaved their souls to the spaceship's cosmic protection began to blink out, one by one.

GARGOYLES

Colleen Anderson

glowers deter aerial attacks
protect edifices and dare the devil's notice
the granite beast's rocky presence wards
places of worship, parapets and rooves
as devotedly plain as a gargoyle
is grotesquely intricate

redoubtable soldiers, ever vigilant
accustomed to nature's onslaught
to spout water from any castle or church
they serve as decoration and defense
stalwart judges to misdeeds

gargoyles look out upon the world
guarding, gazing past the far horizon
for whatever force may descend
it is sure to be forged by strong wills
of gods, devils, or determined men

when called to duty the gargoyle launches
yet its demonic roots work against it
talons dig into buildings, gouge and scar
crumbling masonry and faulty mortaring
begin to yield where battles never breached

to shield humanity's constructs is a lofty goal
yet gradual deterioration and disrepair
erodes the stone monster's reason to be
walls and gargoyles crumble to ruin, succumb
to time, the one enemy neither can defeat

GARGOYLE

Jennifer Weigel

CONTRIBUTORS

Colleen Anderson's poems have been published in such venues as *Mirror Dance*, *Polu Texni*, *The Future Fire*, *HWA Poetry Showcase* and others. She lives in Vancouver, BC and is a Canada Council and BC Arts Council grant recipient for writing and has performed her work before audiences in the US, UK and Canada. Colleen's published fiction can be found in various venues, including the collection *A Body of Work*, Black Shuck Books. Her poetry collection, *I Dreamed a World*, is forthcoming from LVP Publications.

Manuel Arenas is a writer of verse and prose in the Gothic Horror tradition. His work has appeared in *Spectral Realms* and *Penumbra*, both from Hippocampus Press, and in sundry genre anthologies. In 2021 he released his first collection of prose and poetry, *Book of Shadows: Grim Tales and Gothic Fancies*, from Jackanapes Press. He currently resides in Phoenix, Arizona, where he pens his dark ditties sheltered behind heavy curtains, as he shuns the oppressive orb which glares down on him from the cloudless, dust-filled sky.

Bruce Boston's writing has received numerous awards, most visibly, the Bram Stoker Award, a Pushcart Prize, the *Asimov's* Readers Award, and the Rhysling and Grandmaster Awards of the Science Fiction Poetry Association. His latest fiction collection, *Gallimaufry*, is available from Amazon and other online booksellers.

Frank Coffman is a retired professor of English, Creative Writing and Journalism (as well as being the Editor and Publisher of this tome). He has published speculative poetry and fiction in a variety of journals, magazines, anthologies, and collections. Following a chapbook, *This Ae Nighte, Every Nighte and Alle* (2018), he has published three large collections of speculative verse: *The Coven's Hornbook & Other Poems* (2019); *Black Flames & Gleaming Shadows* (2020), and *Eclipse* *of the Moon* (2021). He just published his first collection of short fiction: *Three Against the Dark: Collected Dr. Venn Occult Detective Mysteries* (March 2022). He is a Formalist poet, working with meter and rhyme in cross-cultural, ancient, medieval, exotic, and traditional English forms. Experimentation with "blended" forms—especially variations on the sonnet—form much of his work with structured verse. He is a member of the Horror Writers Association and the Science Fiction and Fantasy Poetry Association. He established and moderates the Weird Poets Society Facebook site.

Scott J. Couturier is a poet & prose writer of the Weird, liminal, & darkly fantastic. His work has appeared in numerous venues, including *The Audient Void, Spectral Realms, Cosmic Horror Monthly, Space and Time Magazine,* & *Weirdbook.* Currently he works as a copy & content editor for Mission Point Press, living an obscure reverie in the wilds of northern Michigan with his partner/live-in editor & two cats. His debut collection of Weird & autumnal verse, *I Awaken In October,* is due out late 2022 from Jackanapes Press.

Harris Coverley has had verse published in *Polu Texni, California Quarterly, Star*Line, Spectral Realms, Scifaikuest, BFS Horizons, Novel Noctule, Corvus Review, The Cannon's Mouth, The Crank, Apocalypse Confidential, View From Atlantis,* and many others. He lives in Manchester, England.

Joshua Gage is an ornery curmudgeon from Cleveland. His newest chapbook, *blips on a screen,* is available on Cuttlefish Books. He is a graduate of the Low Residency MFA Program in Creative Writing at Naropa University. He has a penchant for Pendleton shirts, Ethiopian coffee, and any poem strong enough to yank the breath out of his lungs.

Maxwell I. Gold is a multiple award nominated prose poet and author from Columbus, Ohio. His work focuses primarily on weird and cosmic horror and he has appeared in numerous anthologies and magazines including *Weirdbook Magazine, Space and Time Magazine, Startling Stories, Strange Horizons, Tales from OmniPark Anthology, Shadow Atlas: Dark Landscapes of the Americas* and more. Maxwell also currently serves on the Board of Trustees for the Horror Writers Association as the organization's Treasurer. His debut prose poetry collection *Oblivion in Flux: A Collection of Cyber Prose* was recently released by Crystal Lake Publishing. Read more at www.thewellsoftheweird.com or follow him on instagram @cybergodwrites.

Amelia Gorman is a recent transplant to Eureka, California and you can usually find her walking her dogs or foster dogs in the woods or exploring tide pools. Her fiction has appeared recently in Nightscript 6 and her poetry in *Liminality, Star*Line, Penumbric* and *Vastarien*. Her first chapbook, *Field Guide to Invasive Species of Minnesota*, is available from Interstellar Flight Press. Find her online at:
www.ameliagorman.com

Wendy Harrison is a retired prosecutor who turned to writing short mystery fiction during the pandemic, finding it almost as satisfying to punish the bad guys on paper as it was in real life. Her stories have been published in numerous anthologies including *Peace, Love & Crime, Autumn Noir, CRIMEUCOPIA: Tales from the Front Porch,* and *Death of a Bad Neighbour.* She lives in Florida with her first-reader husband Brooks and Cooper, their Shepherd mix rescue dog.

Patricia Hope's award-winning writing has appeared in *Chicken Soup for the Soul, Number One, Pigeon Parade Quarterly, 2021 Anthology of Appalachian Writers, The Mildred Haun Review, Tiny Seed, Liquid Imagination, American Diversity Report,* and many others. Born and raised in Appalachia, she now lives in Oak Ridge, Tennessee.

Ann Thornfield-Long
Tennessee Women of Vision and Courage, (edited by Crawford and Smiley, 2013) *Artemis Journal, Silver Blade, The Tennessee Magazine, American Diversity Report, Liquid Imagination, Riddled with Arrows, Abyss and Apex, Pigeon Parade Quarterly, Wordgathering*
Patricia Boatner Fiction Award (Tennessee Mountain Writers, 2017) Weymuth residency (2017) Rhysling and Pushcart nominations and Best of the Net nominations

Sherry Poff holds an MA in Writing from the University of Tennessee at Chattanooga and is a member of the Chattanooga Writers' Guild. Her work has appeared recently in *Raconteur Review*, *Heart of Flesh* and *Flash Nonfiction Food* (Woodhall Press). Sherry's short poem "Resurrection" was nominated for the Pushcart Prize.

John C. Mannone has poems in speculative journals such as *Space & Time Magazine*, *Elixir*, *Nebo*, *Eye to the Telescope*, and speculative poems in the literary journals *North Dakota Quarterly*, *Foreign Literary Review*, *Le Menteur*, *Poetry South*, *New England Journal of Medicine*, and others. He won the Dwarf Stars Award (2020) and the HWA Scholarship (2017). Some literary distinctions include: Impressions of Appalachia Creative Arts Contest poetry prize (2020), the Carol Oen Memorial Fiction Prize (2020), and the Joy Margrave Award in nonfiction (2015, 2017). He was awarded a Jean Ritchie Fellowship (2017) in Appalachian literature, two Weymouth writing residencies (2016, 2017), and served as the celebrity judge for the National Federation of State Poetry Societies (2018). His two forthcoming collections are *Flux Lines: The Intersection of Science, Love, and Poetry* (Linnet's Wings Press, 2021) and *Sacred Flute* (Iris Press, 2021/2022). He edits poetry for *Abyss & Apex*, *Silver Blade*, *Liquid Imagination*, and *American Diversity Report*. A retired physics professor, John lives in Knoxville, Tennessee. http://jcmannone.wordpress.com

Lee Murray is a multi-award-winning author-editor and poet from Aotearoa-New Zealand. A double Bram Stoker, and Shirley Jackson Award winner, Lee is a NZSA Honorary Literary Fellow, and Grimshaw Sargeson Fellow for 2021 for her narrative prose-poetry work *Fox Spirit on a Distant Cloud*. Her debut poetry collection, *Tortured Willows: Bent. Bowed. Unbroken*, a collaborative title with Christina Sng, Angela Yuriko Smith, and Geneve Flynn was released in 2021 from Yuriko Publishing. Read more at leemurray.info

Kathryn Reilly By day, Kathryn helps her students investigate words' power. At night, she reads retold myths and sometimes breathes life into new ones. She loves a good poetic adventure. Several anthologies host her works including *Shadow Atlas: Dark Landscapes of the Americas. Sage Cigarettes*, *Last Leaves*, and *Last Girls Club* host recent poetry. Her rescue mutts Savvie and Roxy Razzamatazz hear the stories first. Twitter and Instagram: @katecanwrite

Magnolia Silcox is a nineteen-year-old published author. Her favorite hobbies include writing, hiking,reading and drawing. Her published works often appear in anthologies. She is most known for her works of poetry, nonfiction, drabbles, and short fictional works. She often writes works about her experiences with Schizophrenia. She is a mental health advocate for people living with Schizophrenia. She loves watching anime and listening to dubstep as well. She currently lives in Grants, New Mexico with her family. She lives with her mom, dad, little sister, two little brothers, her dog Mia and her two cats named Ember and Scratch.

Marge Simon lives in Ocala, Florida, with her husband, poet/writer Bruce Boston and the ghosts of two cats. She has three Bram Stoker Awards, Rhysling Awards for Best Long and Best Short Fiction, the Elgin, Dwarf Stars and Strange Horizons Readers' Award. She received HWA's Lifetime Service Award in 2021. Marge's poems and stories have appeared in *Crannog, Bracken, Asimov's, Silver Blade, Journal of Condensed Creative Art, New Myths, Daily Science Fiction*. Her stories also appear in anthologies such as *Tales of the Lake 5, Chiral Mad 4, You, Human and The Beauty of Death*, to name a few. She attends the ICFA annually as a guest poet/writer and is a founding member of the Speculative Literary Foundation. https://www.amazon.com//e/B006G29PL6/ margesimon   website: margesimon.com

Liam A Spinage is a former philosophy student, former archaeology educator and former police clerk who spends most of his spare time on the beach gazing up at the sky and across the sea while his imagination runs riot. Occasionally, this imagination has been known to spill out onto paper. A new writer but an old soul, his writing has been published by *Dyst* literary journal, *Land Beyond the World* magazine and *The Reach* as well as anthologies by Gravestone and Thuggish Itch.

https://www.amazon.co.uk/~/e/B083VVHV41
https://twitter.com/Tweedlesmart

Jay Sturner is a writer, poet, and naturalist from the western suburbs of Chicago. He is the author of several books of poetry and a collection of short stories. His writing has appeared in such publications as *Space and Time Magazine*, *Spectral Realms*, *Not One of Us*, *Star*Line*, and *JOURN-E: The Journal of Imaginative Literature*, among others. Sturner is also a professional birdwalk leader.

Rebecca Thrush has poetry published both in print and online with a variety of journals. Most notably this past year, she was featured to be part of *Viewless Wing's* 2021 *Scary Art Show* and *Line of Advance's* 2021 Wright Award series. She also has original art online with *Decomp Journal* and *Oddball Magazine*.

DJ Tyrer is the person behind *Atlantean Publishing*, editor of *View From Atlantis*, and has been published in *The Rhysling Anthology 2016*, *Speculations III*, and issues of *Enchanted Conversation*, *The Horrorzine*, *Red Planet*, *Scifaikuest*, *Sirens Call*, *Spectral Realms*, *Star*Line*, and *Tigershark*, as well as releasing several chapbooks, such as *The Tears of Lot-49*. The e-chapbook *One Vision* is available from Tigershark Publishing's website. *SuperTrump* and *A Wuhan Whodunnit* are available to download from the Atlantean Publishing website.
DJ Tyrer's website is at https://djtyrer.blogspot.co.uk/
DJ Tyrer's Facebook page is at https://www.facebook.com/DJTyrerwriter/

Kyla Lee Ward is a Sydney-based creative who works in many modes, that have garnered her Australian Shadows and Aurealis awards. She has placed in the Rhyslings and received Stoker and Ditmar nominations. *The Macabre Modern and Other Morbidities* is her second collection of dark and fantastic fiction and poetry after 2011's *The Land of Bad Dreams*. Her short fiction has also appeared in *Weirdbook*, *Shadowed Realms*, and on Gothic.net, and in anthologies such as *Gods, Memes and Monsters: a 21st century Bestiary* and *Oz Is Burning*. Cowritten with her partner under the name Edwina Grey, the novel *Prismatic* won an

Aurealis for Best Horror. Her work on RPGs including *Demon: the Fallen* saw her appear as a guest at the inaugural Gencon Australia. Her short film, 'Bad Reception', screened at the Third International Vampire Film Festival and she is a member of the theatre companies Deadhouse: Tales of Sydney Morgue and The Theatre of Blood, which have also produced her work. Reviewers across all media have accused her of being "gothic and esoteric", "weird and exhilarating" and of "giving me a nightmare." A practising occultist, she likes bats, swordplay and the Hellfire Club. To see some very strange things, try
http://www.tabula-rasa.info

Jennifer Weigel is a multi-disciplinary mixed media conceptual artist. Weigel utilizes a wide range of media to convey her ideas, including assemblage, drawing, fibers, installation, jewelry, painting, performance, photography, sculpture, video and writing. Weigel's art has been exhibited nationally in all 50 states and has won numerous awards. She is also a regular contributor on the horror website Haunted MTL with both art and writing.

Michelle Young has been published in the poetry anthology *Blanket Stories* by Richard Jochum and Ruth Zamoyta, as well as *Festival Writer Issue 2:6 July 2014: Sestinas special issue, American Diversity Report, Quill and Parchment, Crazy Buffet: Curbside Pickup, Silver Blade*, and others. She has participated in readings from *Blanket Stories* at Columbia University and the Princeton Public Library, and enjoys travel that inspires her writing. Michelle and her husband, Corey Green, reside in Chattanooga, Tennessee.

COLOPHON

The body copy is in Goudy Truesdell 13 pt. on 16 pts. of lead.

Bylines are in 14 pt. Goudy Truesdell Bold on 16.

Epigraphs are in Goudy Truesdell 10 pt. on 12.

The Contributors Blurbs are set in Goudy Truesdell
12 point set on 14.4 (normal)

THE FANCY FONT IS ROYAL SIGNAGE

www.ingramcontent.com/pod-product-compliance
Lightning Source LLC
Chambersburg PA
CBHW072040170626
46811CB00008B/3119